Dear Parent:
Your child's love of reading starts here!

Every child learns to read in a different way and at his or her own speed. Some go back and forth between reading levels and read favorite books again and again. Others read through each level in order. You can help your young reader improve and become more confident by encouraging his or her own interests and abilities. From books your child reads with you to the first books he or she reads alone, there are I Can Read Books for every stage of reading:

SHARED READING
Basic language, word repetition, and whimsical illustrations, ideal for sharing with your emergent reader

BEGINNING READING
Short sentences, familiar words, and simple concepts for children eager to read on their own

READING WITH HELP
Engaging stories, longer sentences, and language play for developing readers

READING ALONE
Complex plots, challenging vocabulary, and high-interest topics for the independent reader

ADVANCED READING
Short paragraphs, chapters, and exciting themes for the perfect bridge to chapter books

I Can Read Books have introduced children to the joy of reading since 1957. Featuring award-winning authors and illustrators and a fabulous cast of beloved characters, I Can Read Books set the standard for beginning readers.

A lifetime of discovery begins with the magical words "I Can Read!"

Visit www.icanread.com for information
on enriching your child's reading experience.

I Can Read!™

READING 2 WITH HELP

Silly Street

SELECTED POEMS

by Jeff Foxworthy

pictures by Steve Björkman

HARPER

An Imprint of HarperCollinsPublishers

I Can Read Book® is a trademark of HarperCollins Publishers.

Silly Street: Selected Poems
Copyright © 2009 by Jeff Foxworthy

Library of Congress Cataloging-in-Publication Data is available.
ISBN 978-0-06-176529-2 (trade bdg.) —ISBN 978-0-06-176528-5 (pbk.)

Typography by Rick Farley
10 11 12 13 14   SCP   10 9 8 7 6 5 4 3 2 1

First Edition
Originally published in an unabridged edition by HarperCollins, 2009

To Jordan and Jules:
It is an honor and a joy
being your dad.
—J.F.

For the Hepner family
with great love.
—S.B.

Table of Contents

This Way to Silly Street

Sometimes you're silly

And you know that it's true.

When you're feeling that way,

There are things you can do.

Like jumping in circles

Or spinning around.

Try doing cartwheels

Without falling down.

You could stand on your head

And wiggle your toes,

Or just walk around

With a spoon on your nose.

But if you're looking for more

And want something new,

Then I know a cool place

That's just waiting for you.

Pets-a-Palooza

Pets-a-Palooza

Is a must stop each visit.

You'll find dogs and fat cats

And "Oh my, what is its?"

Maybe the pet that

you seek is a rabbit.

They don't keep them in cages,

So you'll just have to grab it.

Hats and Halos

While on Silly Street

If you yearn for a hat,

You can find what you want

At McDoogle and Pratt.

They have ten thousand hats

And five thousand caps,

Toboggans, tiaras,

Helmets, and wraps.

There are hats for a cowboy

And crowns for a king

And halos for angels

To wear when they sing.

Magic

There used to be a magic store

Run by a man with a beard,

But he pulled out his wand

And gave it a wave

And "poof"

the whole store disappeared!

Bubble Gum Tree

There used to be a bubble gum tree

On the corner of Silly and White.

But the birds picked it clean,

'Twas a sight to be seen.

There were crows

blowing bubbles in flight.

House of Clocks

At Mel's House of Clocks

They only sell socks,

Which makes me ask,

"What was Mel thinking?"

He says, "Socks are the thing

That makes the world sing,

'Cause they're warm and keep

Your feet from stinking!"

Phil's Fluffy and Light

At Phil's Giant Pancakes

Business is slow.

They've sold only one

As far as I know.

It was fluffy and light

And the taste! You can't beat it.

But it took four hundred people

A whole year to eat it.

Feeling Silly

If you're feeling silly,
And you know that you are,
You should buy a balloon
From old Gavin McGarr.

He has some that are long
And some that are round.
There are some you can ride
And fly all over town.

Butterflies

One thing you must see

Is the butterfly tree

Where thousands of butterflies light.

Their wings look like leaves

As they flap in the breeze.

When they leave,

   it's a rainbow in flight.

Perpetual Puddle

If you should stop at Perpetual Puddle,

When you're finished jumping,

    the water and mud'll

    cover your clothes

    and be in your hair.

Your mother will scream

    and people will stare.

Mister Billy

On the street that is Silly

Lives a lady named Tillie.

She has a pet goat

She calls Mister Billy.

Billy is famous for all that he eats.

He'll eat up your socks

And he'll eat pickled beets.

He's eaten my shoes and even a jar.

He once tried to chew up

    a yellow sports car.

27

Pigeon Lady

The pigeon lady

Is known as Ms. Snerds.

She sits on a bench

And sings to the birds.

She gives them her popcorn,

Her crackers and bread.

The pigeons adore her.

They sit on her head.

Pogostick Pete

Pogostick Pete

Never stops hopping.

He hops while he's shaving

And hops when he's shopping.

He hops when he's happy.

He hops when he's blue.

And if you get in his way,

He'll just hop over you.

Silly Street, Again

At the end of the day,

At the end of the street,

You're sure to be smiling.

You're sure to be beat.

And you'll know in your heart

If it's sunny or chilly,

There's a place you can go

If you need to be silly.